102 85

D1416453

HAIRY TUESDAY

Published in the United States of America in 1999
by **MONDO Publishing**

Copyright © 1998 Beltz Verlag, Weinheim und Basel
Programm Beltz & Gelberg, Weinheim

For information contact:
MONDO Publishing
One Plaza Road
Greenvale, New York 11548
MONDO is a registered trademark of Mondo Publishing
Visit our web site at http://www.mondopub.com

Printed in Hong Kong
99 00 01 02 03 04 05 06   HC   9 8 7 6 5 4 3 2 1
99 00 01 02 03 04 05 06   PB   9 8 7 6 5 4 3 2 1

Adapted from the German *Der haarige Dienstag*
English adaptation by Pamela D. Pollack
Designed by Mina Greenstein
Production by The Kids at Our House

Library of Congress Cataloging-in-Publication Data
Orlev, Uri, 1931-
Hairy Tuesday / Uri Orlev ; illustrated by Jacky Gleich.
p.   cm.
An adaptation of Der haarige Dienstag by Pamela D. Pollack.
Summary: Three-year-old Michael hates having his hair washed in
the bathtub every Tuesday night, a time when he cries and cries.
ISBN 1-57255-651-X . — ISBN 1-57255-652-8 (pbk. : alk. paper)
[1. Hair—Care and hygiene—Fiction.] I. Gleich, Jacky, ill. II. Title.
PZ7.0633Hai   1999
[Fic]—dc21   98-50375   CIP   AC

HAIRY TUESDAY

by Uri Orlev

illustrated by Jacky Gleich

Every morning, as soon as he opened his eyes, Michael wanted to know what day it was. He jumped out of bed and turned on the radio.

He hoped it wasn't Tuesday.

Every Tuesday Michael had his hair washed.

Michael was afraid of having his hair washed. Sometimes the water was too hot or too cold. Sometimes soap got in his eyes or bubbles got in his nose.

When Michael washed his stuffed bunny's hair, his bunny Pepper didn't seem afraid.

Some Tuesday mornings Michael came
to breakfast wearing a hat. But Mom always
remembered his hair was underneath.
   "I don't want my hair washed," Michael
announced.

"He's only three years old," said Michael's sister Daniella. "Maybe he doesn't need to have his hair washed."

Daniella was eight years old and wasn't afraid of having her hair washed.

But on Tuesday evenings Michael was always in the bathtub having his hair washed. Some Tuesdays he cried so loudly it sounded like a sea monster was in the tub.

Dad and Daniella peeked into the bathroom.

"When I'm a mother, I'll never wash my kid's hair," said Daniella.

"Really!" said Mom.

"Maybe you could just rub his head with a washcloth," Dad suggested.

"That wouldn't get the jam out, or the peanut butter, or the sand from the playground," said Mom.

So Michael had his hair washed every Tuesday no matter how hard he cried.

Each week the noise seemed to get worse.

Dad tried to help. He sang Michael songs from the hallway. He made funny noises. But Michael just cried and cried.

Daniella stuck her fingers in her ears and kept them there the whole time. Sometimes Dad went fishing.

One night Daniella had an idea.

"Michael," she whispered when they were in bed. "Would you like never to have your hair washed again?"

Michael's eyes got very wide. "Yes," he answered.

"Okay," said Daniella. "Tomorrow we'll go to the barber and ask him to cut off all your hair."

Daniella giggled in the dark. Now there would be nothing for Mom to wash on Tuesdays.

"Will it hurt?" asked Michael.

"Not at all," Daniella promised.

The next afternoon Daniella took Michael to Sammy's Barber Shop. Daniella held Michael's hand and Michael held Pepper.

"My brother needs a haircut," Daniella announced to Sammy. "Actually, he needs all his hair cut off."

"Does he have gum in his hair?" Sammy asked.

"Not exactly," said Daniella as she and Michael sat down to wait.

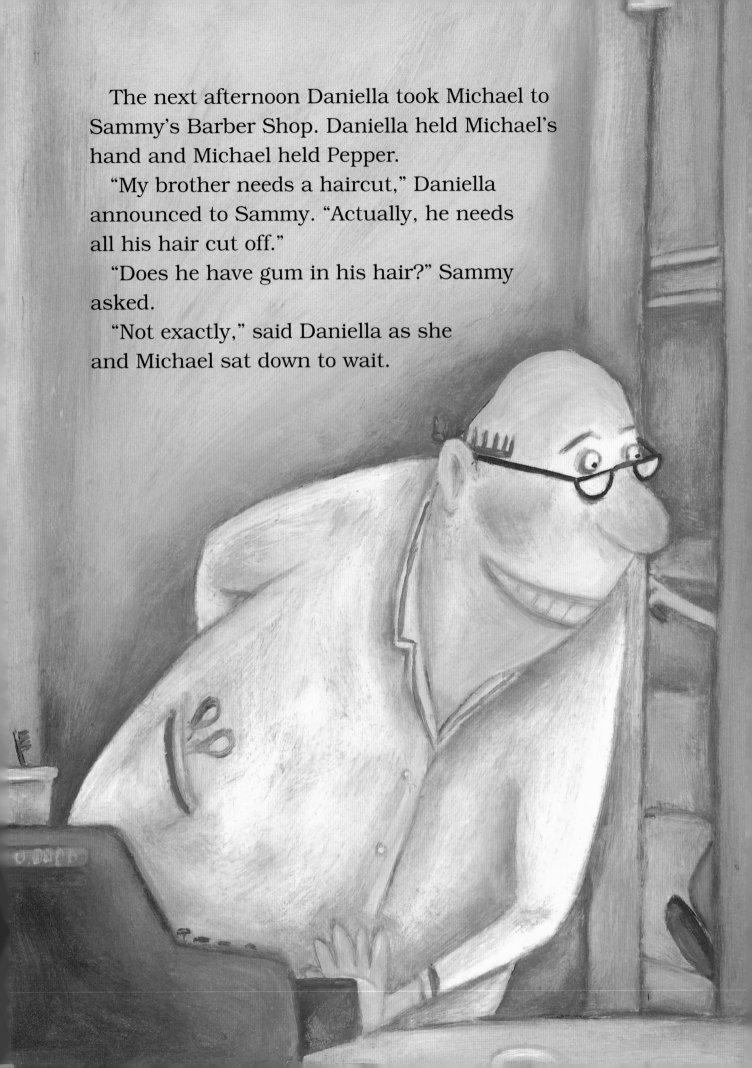

Another little boy was in the barber's chair. The boy's mother sat close by giving Sammy directions.

"Make it shorter," she said. "Make it a little shorter than that. Just a little shorter."

"Do you want *all* his hair cut off?" Sammy asked.

"Of course not, Sammy," said the boy's mother.

Click, click, click went Sammy's scissors and the boy's hair piled up on the floor. Michael clutched Pepper and leaned toward Daniella.

"I want to go home," Michael whispered in Daniella's ear.

"But it's Tuesday," Daniella whispered back.

"I don't care," Michael said softly. "I want to go home."

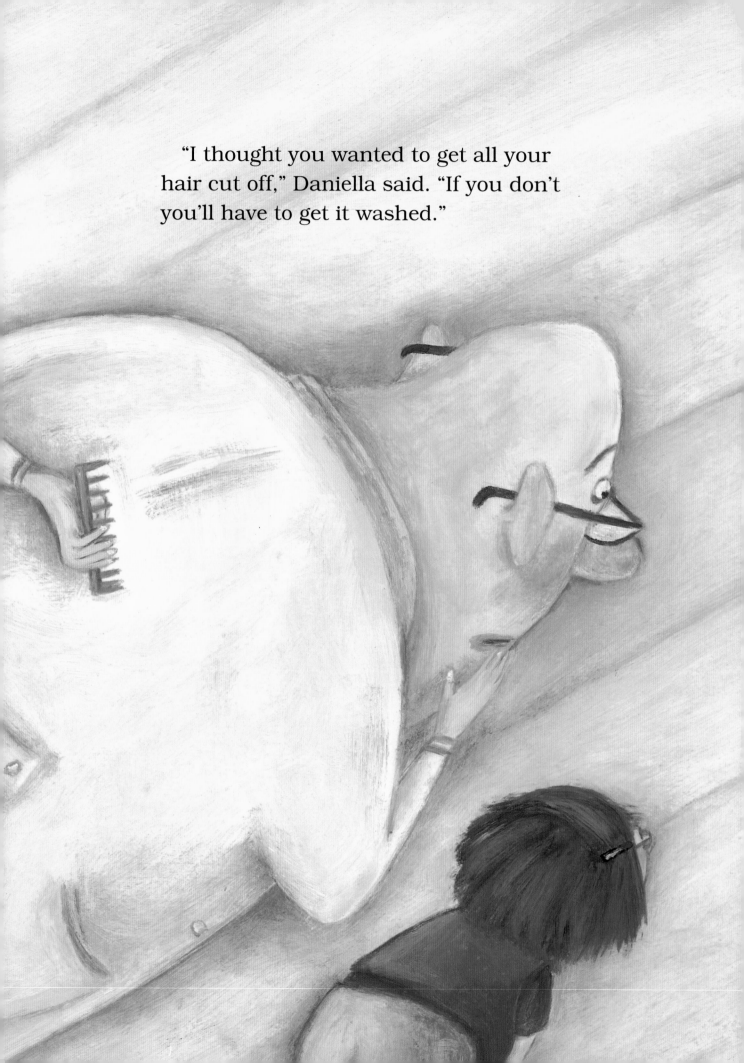

"I thought you wanted to get all your
hair cut off," Daniella said. "If you don't
you'll have to get it washed."

Everyone looked at Michael.
Michael's eyes filled with tears.
"I want to go home," he sobbed.

Daniella took Michael's hand and Michael grabbed Pepper. They walked home.

"It's Tuesday," Daniella reminded Michael. "Mom will wash your hair tonight."

"I know," said Michael. "But I want to keep my hair where it is."

"But you'll cry again," said Daniella.

"No I won't," said Michael.

"I bet you will," said Daniella.

That night Michael told his mother,
"I'm not going to cry in the bathtub."
"That would be nice," said Mom.
"If you don't cry we'll get you a special
surprise for being so brave."

But when it was time to have his hair washed, Michael cried as usual. The noise was not quite as loud, but it lasted longer because he had lost his surprise, too.

"Don't worry," said Mom. "You can get your special surprise any time you let me wash your hair without crying."

"You cried again," Daniella said to Michael
when he was in bed.

"I know," said Michael.

"Are you going to keep crying every Tuesday?"
asked Daniella.

"No," said Michael. "I'm just going to keep
crying until I stop."

And that is exactly what he did.

This is the special present Michael got from Mom, Dad, and Daniella as soon as he stopped crying when his hair was washed on Tuesdays. He was three and a half years old.

What do you think it was?